About the Author

Scientist, writer, yoga practitioner, and avid traveler. When not working, she's busy exploring the world.

What Women Want: A Pocket Guide to Navigating Online Dating

Polina Zaytseva

What Women Want: A Pocket Guide to Navigating Online Dating

Olympia Publishers
London

www.olympiapublishers.com
OLYMPIA PAPERBACK EDITION

Copyright © Polina Zaytseva 2022

The right of Polina Zaytseva to be identified as author of
this work has been asserted in accordance with sections 77 and 78
of the Copyright, Designs and Patents Act 1988.

All Rights Reserved

No reproduction, copy or transmission of this publication
may be made without written permission.
No paragraph of this publication may be reproduced,
copied or transmitted save with the written permission of the
publisher, or in accordance with the provisions
of the Copyright Act 1956 (as amended).

Any person who commits any unauthorised act in relation to
this publication may be liable to criminal
prosecution and civil claims for damage.

A CIP catalogue record for this title is
available from the British Library.

ISBN: 978-1-80074-875-0

The information in this book has been compiled by way of general
guidance only. Neither the author nor the publisher shall be liable or
responsible for any loss or damage allegedly arising from any
information or suggestion in this book.

First Published in 2022

Olympia Publishers
Tallis House
2 Tallis Street
London
EC4Y 0AB

Printed in Great Britain

Dedication

To my parents

Acknowledgements

Carol, thank you, for giving me the idea of writing a book. I admire your sense of humor and happy spirit.
I wish to express particular thanks to the team at Olympia Publishers in London.
Above all, thank you, Liza, Steph and Masha. I am grateful to have you in my life.

We live in a fast paced, busy and evolving world. These days, men and women do not necessarily end up marrying the girl/guy next door, like our parents did. We prefer to travel the world, explore the opportunities, go on voyages and have some fun before settling down.

In the last decade, online dating has surged, initially not being taken seriously, it is nowadays one of the main ways people find their partners.

Online dating has brought many happy couples together. At the same time, it has led to many people feeling frustrated they are not matching with who they want to match with. The dates they have don't lead to where they would like it to. Those people pronounce the whole online dating messed up, stay away from it and declare they are happily single.

I myself have scrolled through dating apps feeling frustrated I am not attracted to what I am seeing online. I have gone on dates only to be disappointed.

One night, while having dinner with a friend and telling her of yet another too bad to be true joke a guy said to me online and how it made me lose interest, she exclaimed I should write a book on online dating. And this is how this book came about.

First impressions matter. Especially in online dating, with thousands of profiles available at your fingertips, and research showing it takes us a split second to decide on the potential of the future mate. After doing extensive review of the men profiles on dating apps, I realized I could help them be better at this game. Help them get the online match they want, tell them what they are doing wrong and why the ladies don't match them, make the dating lives of people more exciting, and reveal what is it that women want in online dating.

There are hundreds of books written out there for women. We are told how to dress better, how to behave, how to catch the guy, and we go out there, we buy expensive make up, we diet and exercise and look great, only to look around and not find anyone we want to be with. Has anyone spoken to the men out there, and told them what we want?

Have you found yourself feeling frustrated you are not meeting the woman of your dreams through online dating platforms? Have you found yourself not matching with the women you swiped right for? Have you found yourself going on dates only to be disappointed in the outcome and giving up on this whole online dating? If you answered yes to any of the questions, then this guide is for you.

This is a book, written by a woman for men, to finally give answers to what is it that women want. This is a guide intended to help men set the scene, to create the introduction chapter in their romance. Writing the romance story, is of course entirely up to them. Disclaimer: this book is based on experience of selected number of individuals and is for informational purposes only. All names have been changed, and cases are given as mere examples.

Chapter 1:
The online profile

The key message: "The first step toward greatness is to be honest, says the proverb; but the proverb fails to state the case strong enough. Honesty is not only "the first step toward greatness," — it is greatness itself." — Christian Nestell Bovee

First things first, let's start with the profile itself.

Name
Unless you are hiding from the Interpol, or from your wife, in which cases don't get this book, there is no other motive for you to put a fake name. If more people were able to get to know each other on anonymous web forums under the names Shopgirl and NY152, online dating platforms wouldn't have surged. There is a reason online dating sites require you to list your legal first name in the profile and not your nickname or username. It's called establishing trust. The trust is a fragile matter that is easily broken. You will likely tell your match your real name on the first date anyway, so who are you hiding from? A woman matches with a guy called Max, but in the first conversation he tells her, he is in fact called Alex. Mm okay, you can't put such a simple thing as your name

truthfully; can we actually trust you with other information about you, such as your job and marital status? If celebrities can put down their real names on dating sites, so can you. It is a turn off, when a guy cannot own up to being on a dating site and is pretending to be someone else. If you are scared your colleagues and friends will see you online, it's best you try other ways to meet a girl.

In the case you don't put an actual name at all, and use Mr Hot, or Mr Right or whatever Mr on the profile, you are probably only looking for a quick hook up, and I wonder still if there are any women who'd go for that.

Age
Same thing as the name. Get it right and real. Your profile says your age is 38, and in your description you write the app has messed it up and your actual age is 33/43/53. If you can't even set the age right, how are we supposed to trust you get other matters in order?

Profile description
Yes, we do want to see *your* character in the description. However, if you are not the creative type, who can produce something catchy, keep it short, simple and friendly. A couple of sentences, a brief statement of your interests, a few emojis will suffice. We aren't here to read philosophical opuses. Refrain from stating that you are funny in the profile description. First of all, not everybody has the same sense of humor, and second, if that is the case, show it off with your punchlines instead of making flat, boring statements. Some men out there proclaim that they are looking for an interesting and

attractive match. The last time I checked, that's what we are all here for. I have yet to meet a person who was searching for a boring and an ugly match.

Height. Please do include it and save yourself the wasted time going on pointless dates with a woman a head taller than you. If you both don't mind the height difference, there is nothing wrong with that, but then a lot of people do mind. Save the time for both of you. Also, to the guys who round up to "180 cm" but are a few cm short in reality — we *see* you. It will not go unnoticed.

Job description. Ok we get it, you work for Secret Intelligence Services and do not wish to disclose your job online on your profile for the whole world to see. Then just do not include anything. Statements like "working with something that's none of your business" is a sign of disrespect to us all. Yes, it is none of our business as for now you are an anonymous online profile, but you do wish to get to know the person behind the profile, don't you? In that case you are referring this statement to them directly.

Avoid the nerdy questions in the profile description such as "what is the most disgusting dessert you ever had?" — you really want her to think of something gross before messaging a complete stranger? Low expectations indeed. Why can't you ask instead "what is the best dessert you ever had?"

Please, please avoid the unoriginal statements about yourself one sees all over the Internet.

"My mother thinks I'm cute and funny" — yes, your mother has great taste, no one is arguing, but taste is subjective.

"Rated 5 stars by Beyonce" — in which case, why

aren't you with Beyonce?

"Looking for my Tinderella" — outdated and unoriginal by now.

Aside from the unoriginal pronouncements, for your own sake, avoid the depressing ones. Dating and meeting people is supposed to be fun and easygoing, no pressure. The idea is to attract the person on the other side to your profile, and not to repel them. Statements like "I could offer a guided tour through Paris, teach you to play the guitar, too bad I live in the middle-of-nowhere, and don't know how to play" will not get you far. What do you want to achieve with this message? Are you indirectly asking the future match of yours to walk you through Paris and teach you to play the guitar, or are you hoping she would be attracted to the fact that you do not seem to offer much? I hope that now after reading this to yourself, you realize how depressing this sounds.

If you are not in the mood to have some fun with a girl and make her laugh, get off the dating app and do something else instead. Play sports, make music, feel better, and only then get back in the game. It is like on the plane in case of emergency — put the oxygen mask on yourself first, before assisting others, i.e., make sure you feel good and happy yourself first, before charming others.

One more slip that is often frowned upon, in your description you are telling a girl what to do. "Big girls, stand tall and proud" — who said anything to suggest they are not standing tall and proud? And why should we listen to an online profile telling us what to do anyway? These condescending statements will mostly make us laugh and hope for you that you realize this one day, before swiping left never to see this profile again.

Images

Down to business. To the most important representative part of the whole profile.

They say a picture is worth a thousand words. The first photo one sees on the dating platform is generally the decisive make or break one. It takes seconds for us to evaluate a person's appearance and decide if it is a yes or no. If it is not a definite no, and she is somehow interested in seeing more, she will scroll to the next photos, and then decide, but as a general rule, the first photo is key, so make it a good one. Please do turn to us and face us on the first image. Yes, great to see the sexy back on that climbing photo, but we want to see the cute face and the cheeky smile first.

If your job isn't being James Bond and working for Secret Intelligence Services, saving the world from villains, skip the mysterious look on the first photo. Do glance into the camera lens in at least one of the images. If you seem to be staring at the sky/at the ground/at your phone on all of your photos, it makes us wonder if you would be able to focus on us at all.

Smile. It's that simple. Happy smile. The corners of your lips should be turned upwards, and not downwards. If you look gloomy on the photos, for whatever reason you decided to upload them, I assume you are going through a rough phase in life and swipe left (no, that look doesn't make me want to cheer you up). You are trying to sell yourself here and tell the future date why she should want you. Act like a Happy Meal, and not an expired one from yesterday, but a still edible one.

Try to keep your accessories such as huge coffee mugs, umbrellas, books, scarfs, hats, surgical masks away from your face on the pictures. Face coverings serve as physiological and physical safety barriers, and understandably, some of us instinctively are trying to shield against stares and judgements of our clothes and appearance. The world of online dating can be a harsh, judgmental place, but hiding away from it is unlikely to benefit you. Just own up to what you have.

Lighting and focus. Well-lit, bright and sharp images where you are in focus, clearly visible and not hiding somewhere in the background, please. I am not swiping right or left on the green bushes.

Please avoid the following images to make the best impression on your online dating profile:

- Bathroom selfies. Somebody had to say it. Can we please ban the bathroom selfies from the online dating platforms? Yes, you do look great in that one photo, the only turn off is that toilet bowl I am seeing to the left of you. What's next — a selfie of you sitting on that aforementioned toilet bowl? Kind of makes us wonder, do you not possess a couple of photos that do not include hygiene equipment?
- Pillow photos. I assume you are only looking for hookups or you are too lazy to search through your phone for images/go outside and take some.
- Sticking out your tongue. Unless you are below the age of 16, please put your tongue back in your mouth and keep it shut.
- Try to avoid using the corporate headshots. Yes, you have probably spent a ton of money on that one

formal photo, but keep it for LinkedIn though. This isn't a business networking event. The women have unanimously voted no on those images.

- A photo of yourself with a cropped out female next to you. Yes — we can see the long hair on your shoulder, and no, that's not appealing. Whether it is a former relationship or not, avoid uploading those images.
- Photos in a group of women. Let me just ask, what message are you trying to convey here? I have to say, we are not particularly attracted to you in these photos. Yes, great, you have many women friends, why aren't you dating one of them? If the women don't seem to look like your friends, but merely there posing for a photo, such as, they are dressed up performers at an event, that's even more unattractive to the potential future matches in the online world. I wonder, would the men approve, if women posted pictures of themselves surrounded by a rugby team?
- Group picture for a first photo. Are you unsure of yourself and hiding behind your friends? Why should I be looking out for you in a crowd full of people on the first image?

One photo, however, is definitely not enough to make a good impression, and ideally it should be 4–5 images. The principle is the same: well-lit, sharp images, where you are clearly visible, your happy face showing on most photos. It is best to upload photos from different activities/life events to display your character, otherwise a profile with 4–5 headshots taken from different angles may look boring and suggest one does not have anything interesting to offer.

It is best to own up to what you have. If Mother Nature has spared you a head full of golden locks, do not try to hide it with caps and hats, otherwise it may come as a surprise to your date later on and backfire against you.

Some people would like to display their photographic artwork, humor or pictures of food, and instead of putting images of themselves, they use the space to show off the photographs they took, the memes they found funny or the sushi rolls they made. This isn't the space. This is the space and the opportunity to show off yourself, how you are and where you are. If a woman is interested in you physically, she would be happy to know more about your photographic artwork. No woman I have spoken to was attracted to a photo of a frog in the profile.

Chapter 2:
The dress code guide

The key message: "You can never be overdressed or overeducated." — Oscar Wilde

Yes, we get it, most of you busy men hate shopping. However, a man's style can make or break the first impression. If you are unsure whether your dress style suits you, or you want to up your game, acquire a copy of the latest GQ, ask for a friend's suggestions, or get a personal shopper, who will help to create a wardrobe appropriate for your body type and age. In short, always go for high quality fabrics and good fit. The advice I have compiled here is classic and timeless, and it certainly works well to this day.

On the neat appearance. Not to sound like your mother, but appearance *is* important. Establishing a grooming routine can only benefit you. Comb your hair, fight dandruff, cut your nails, brush your teeth, wear a deodorant and wash your clothes. (True first date horror story: attempted French kiss with the worst bad breath, need I say there was never a second date?) Don't overdo on that hair gel. All men need to know of and implement these personal hygiene habits if they want others to be attracted to them. (And yes, please get rid of that goatee!

No, you are not AJ from the Backstreet Boys. Facial hair should be either full-on, or non-existent).

When it comes to the dress code, one of the most important rules here is to dress your age. A twenty-year-old guy in a custom-made cashmere suit that's worth a month's salary is looking equally strange as a fifty-year-old guy in ripped jeans and crystal embellished T-shirt. (In fact, get rid of that attire as soon as you hit the 30+ category). There is appropriate timing for everything: while young men's style can pretty well get away with screaming "look at me", men in the professional category (30+) best stay with classy elegance.

A suit. Every man should own one tailored, well-fit suit made of high-quality fabrics. Obviously, a car mechanic does not need to have a collection of suits, as an attorney does. However, one suit should be present in everyone's wardrobe, intended for the interviews, festivities and business meetings. Ensure the pants have proper length. A classic style for pants goes for no break in front and back. If your ankles are visible, the pants are too short. Ties should be made of good quality fabrics. Ties made of linen and cotton fabric are lightweight, while wool and knitted ties are practical and sturdy. However, the ultimate fabric for a well-dressed professional look would be silk.

For casual style, a pair of dark blue, well-fitted jeans always works, and can be considered a good investment (so grab a couple). Pair it up with T-shirts and shirts of all kinds.

A navy blue blazer suits all ages, goes with anything, and is a perfect look for business casual attire or for pairing up with printed shirts for a cheeky smart casual date look.

They say good shoes take you to good places. Spend money on shoes. Well-made shoes of high-quality look good, last longer and may just as well be more comfortable than the cheap mass-market ones. Essential shoes for men include the brogues, the loafers, the minimalist sneakers, and the Derby. Black colored shoes are classy and formal, while brown are versatile and can be worn on any occasion.

Invest wisely in a nice watch. Yes, indeed, you can check the time on your smartphone, however, besides having to reach in the pocket for your gadget all the time, a watch gets points for being a timeless accessory. It is a subtle detail, but people (read: women) notice it. Get one that fits well with your personality, whether you are a sporty guy or are into art and graphic design. A classic, well-made watch is like a classic well-made car; it will still look good decades from now. A watch is a personal, functional and aesthetic accessory, it will always be there for you, just like our ancestors have always equipped themselves with talismans for luck and protection.

Items to avoid

If the advice above has not resonated with you or seems like too much effort, please be sure to remove the following items from your wardrobe/online profile (otherwise, you are risking a prompt swipe to the left and out of sight):

- Baggy pants. A huge no and one of the worst fashion mistakes ever. Get rid of the oversized and baggy

pants and give them to charity.
- Men's cargo pants. Nothing flattering or appealing in that garment with massive pockets — they only make you look bulky.
- Long T-shirts. Unless you are a hip-hop music artist, consider giving them away.
- Heavy print T-shirts — went out of style just about 5 years ago.
- Side-cut tank tops. No, the online dating profile is not the gym or your Sunday DIY project.
- Skinny jeans or ultra-tight-fitting pants. No, they do not showcase your body in the best light.
- The finger-shoes. While these may not be noticeable on the profile, please be sure to never show up to a date spotting a pair of these. Ever.
- Formal shoes with pointy toes. Get rid of them, this isn't the 1990s any more.
- Wearing sunglasses indoors (and taking pictures with them on for the online dating profile), no dude, not cool, more like wannabe cool.
- Speed dealer sunglasses. Should be a long-forgotten fashion trend by now, yet some people just do not wish to let it go.
- Skip the stripy scarf on your pictures. Unless you are over 60 years of age, please remove those photos, you know who you are. No girl I've spoken to was attracted to a stripy scarf. Get rid of the photos, and even better, give the scarf away to your grandpa.
- Untucked dress shirts. No, they do not make the look more casual. They make it look unorganized and messy, as if you had crashed on a friend's couch the night

before.

- Avoid the bright red shiny ties with black shirts. Shiny fabrics look cheap and flashy, and should not be worn, let alone paired with a suit.
- Similarly, it's a no-go for black shirt with white tie. Unless you work in the food service industry as a waiter, this combination should not be worn. A black shirt should only be paired with a black tie.

Chapter 3:
The initial online conversations

The key message: "Etiquette...means behaving yourself a little better than is absolutely essential." —Will Cuppy.

According to Wikipedia, a pick-up line is intended to open a conversation in order to engage a person for romance or dating. The key word here is *engage*. One cute pick-up line sometimes is all you need to break the ice and get the girl's attention. Consider this one purely for study purposes here: "Hey, here I am, what are your other two wishes?" First of all, it's friendly, as one puts themselves at your disposal. It's creative, as it gets the girl to think of something pleasant she would like, and we all like to think of pleasant things. It's also cocky, but who said confidence wasn't attractive?

How to start the first conversation
The name. Call her by her name. Should be a known by now, but somehow it isn't. Spelled out by Dale Carnegie in the last century, the person's name is the sweetest sound to their ears. Yet so many people prefer to just say "Hi" "Hey" "Hey girl" "Hey lady" "Hey pretty lady" in the very first conversation. No.

By calling her by her name as the very first opening line, you are showing that you are looking at the person behind the online profile. Down the line, of course, you greet however you want, but the initial message is important to show her your interest. (Also, would be great if you could extend the name-calling to live conversations.)

One nice way to start a conversation is to ask your match something about herself based on the profile, as people love talking about themselves. Check out her photos and ask her how she liked Paris, should there be a picture of her in front of the Eiffel Tower.

If you cannot think of playful, original ways to start a conversation, just compliment her. Tell her she has a beautiful smile/nice photos/cool profile. Open up with simple questions, such as how are you doing, how is your day? Yes, those are generic questions, and obviously, the person responding might not necessarily tell the truth. However, these questions are friendly, easy going, and do not require a lot of effort to answer. And it's good to start off easy. The key is then to ask the match the follow-up questions and slowly build a connection.

How <u>not</u> to start a conversation
You are scrolling through her profile, wondering how can you stand out, be funny and grab her attention among all the other guys that message her. You see a photo of her on a tennis court with a tennis racket. "Bingo" you think and text her "Hey, did someone put a tennis racket in your hands for a photo or do you actually play tennis?" Ha ha, this is so hilarious, I just fell off my chair laughing. Not.

Hold on a moment and think. Would belittling a woman make her giggle? Would you find it amusing, if a woman messaged you "Hey, did you climb behind the steering wheel for a photo or do you actually know how to drive?" Belittling someone as the first conversation starter (and generally), when you do not know the person behind the online profile is not, I repeat, *is not* funny. Put her on a pedestal instead. Ask her how is the training for Australia Open going, say hi Miss Sharapova, be cute and cheeky and a gentleman.

Avoid starting the chat with sending out your life statement as a first message. "Hey, my name is ___, I am from___, I do this and this, I am ambitious, open-minded, reliable and empathetic. In my spare time I like to go to the gym, read, and cook, what about you?" You are not a potential employee looking for a job, and she isn't the HR. Besides, it puts pressure to have to respond in the same way and at times, it feels like too much effort to reply to all these identical texts. The idea is to engage a person on the other side, and not to offer them yourself in the first message. Our smartphones and gadgets are also reliable, and are there for us 24/7, why do we need you as well?

In the case she does not get back to you, please avoid sending out upset texts, such as "are you speechless?" Maybe she didn't have the time to answer, maybe she changed her mind. Your whining will not rescue it. If you want to get her attention, wish her a good day, ask her how she is doing or invite her for a coffee. Should there still be no answer — move on.

If you do not know how to compliment a girl, watch

some classic movies, TV series, search online "how to compliment a girl" — there were over 300 helpful suggestions on the Internet last time I checked. Just FYI "you are gorgeous" was number one of them. Look at the profile photos and think whom you are trying to compliment. Messaging a woman below 60 years of age in the first conversation "you are like fine wine, only getting better with age" is *not* a compliment.

Questions to avoid
"What are you looking for?"

Occasionally, some of you choose to skip the uncertainty stage of getting to know one another and jump directly to the point, by asking this question and stating you are looking for a relationship. Let me tell you a secret. As a man, you have the control lever in the beginning of establishing a contact. Although times are changing, it is still considered the norm for the man to ask a woman out on the first date. Thus, as a man, you have all the chances to go out there and woo that pretty lady, so she falls in love and in the relationship. So why are you asking that question — in order to deduce whether taking this woman out on dates would be worth it financially? The question is a mood killer. And even if the answer to that question is "relationship", it does not necessarily mean that relationship would be with you, until you attract her somehow. Here is a quote from a paper "The (Perceived) Meaning of Spontaneous Thoughts" in the Journal of Experimental Psychology (1): "Participants felt more sexually attracted to an attractive person whom they thought of spontaneously than deliberately. And reported their commitment to a current romantic relationship would be more affected by the spontaneous rather than deliberate recollection of a good or bad experience with their romantic partner." In other words, we are all looking for attraction, spark and love, however, if you try to force it by asking the "what are you looking for" question, the sex appeal is diminished. Just be spontaneous, embrace uncertainty, and see where this journey goes. Once a connection is established, then it is time to have a conversation as to who are you for each other.

"What are your hobbies?" "What are your passions?"

Yes, when you are looking for a partner, it is important to find someone with some shared common interests, and have things you two would love to do together. But here is a million-dollar question, can you find out the girl's preferred ways to spend her free time without asking those boring, cliché, unoriginal questions? Can you ask her what she likes to do on her weekends? What she would rather be doing on this rainy Wednesday evening?

This question pops up in the majority of conversations. How much fun do we have giving the same answer to different people after a while? I have started coming up with random responses, such as I am collecting stamps (spoiler alert: I'm not), just to avoid typing the same thing all the time.

If the girl is a professional ice skater in her free time and is training for the Olympics, she will likely have photos on her profile and you can ask directly and specifically about that, or she will tell you herself. In other cases, yes, we all like to spend time with our friends, watch movies, listen to music, travel, read books, be in nature to one extent or the other, play sports, and eat good food. You ask a generic boring question, she will likely give you a generic answer.

And why are you asking anyway? If you are looking for a cycling partner, you can ask directly if she is into cycling. Otherwise, here is a secret nobody tells — not all of our hobbies have to match. If you love horse riding and she enjoys art galleries on weekends, isn't it great to have separate interests, to be able to learn from each other and introduce a new activity to your partner? It is so much more important to first match the life principles and beliefs, the sense of humor, to find out if you like the way the other person holds themselves than asking this boring question just for the sake of asking it.

Making assumptions

- "Hey, would you like to have dinner with me in the next couple of days?"
- "Hey, that would be nice, I am too busy this week unfortunately, maybe next week?"
- "Sure, see you next week then. You'll have the time to finish that book you are reading and tell me about it."

Every time you tell a woman you just met what your assumptions are of her or of her time, or what she should be doing, a little bird jumps off a cliff somewhere. You are not our partner yet, neither our boss, nor our schoolteacher. Would be a lot nicer, if you simply said you are looking forward to hearing more about the book she is reading. Just keep in mind that some people, when being told what to do by someone they barely know, instinctively may want to do the opposite to your orders.

Why do some of you guys like making assumptions about us? Is that a matter of trying to own the situation, to make a mental model, as if you know who we are? You tell yourself a fact, without having any evidence to it, and yes, we do find it annoying. Assumptions have been shown to limit our capacity in relating to other people. If you always assume what others do, how they think and feel, you are at risk of not listening and communicating, which later on may leave others feeling misunderstood and affect your relationship.

If in the online profile it states the woman is in "postgraduate education", why do some of you feel the need to ask what is she studying for her Masters degree? It could be Masters, or it could be a Certificate, a Diploma, an Internship, a PhD. Why not just ask, what are you studying? If she tells you she is studying programming, consider not telling her what she is doing, such as "you have to study hard". Maybe she does, maybe she does not. Maybe she is working part time to support herself instead, maybe she is the genius of programming who does not need to study all weekend long, and spends her time doing sports instead. Do you see the difference between "you have to study hard" and "are you studying a lot?" You do not know this person, leave your judgements and assumptions aside and ask her a question instead.

Chapter 4:
The first date and beyond

The key message: "To be a gentleman does not depend upon the tailor or the toilet. Good clothes are not good habits. A gentleman is just a gentle-man — no more, no less; a diamond polished, that was first a diamond in the rough." — William Croswell Doane

You two set the date and time for the first date, congrats! A couple of hours beforehand you realize you could make it to the meeting place 15 minutes earlier. You are looking forward to seeing her, so which message do you send?

(a) Hey, you can come 15 min earlier, I finished work.

(b) Hey, I've finished work already, shall be there in 15, in case you are around.

If you chose the answer (b) well done, you can keep reading. If you chose the answer (a), you might want to look outside and check which century we are living in. We are not your housewives sitting at home, waiting for your message, having nothing better to do than to wait for the time you are set free, so we can meet you. Please, please respect us and our time and check with us, when we can make it to the meeting, instead of telling us what to do.

When it comes to the date itself, first impressions matter. Humans are made to size each other up quickly. We evaluate a person on their appearance in a couple of seconds and form an opinion on the way they are dressed and the way they behave. When you are going on a first date (or to any meeting in life, really), it is of utmost importance to appear in good humour, confident and relaxed. If you are nervous beforehand, take a shot of vodka (a shot is okay, a bottle is a no-no). If you appear looking tired, tense or stressed for whatever reason, it will definitely show, and if you do not seem to want to snap out of it during the date, it will negatively affect the outcome. A busy, no-time-wasting woman will leave the date as soon as she can, a nice girl might stick around for a bit, but that does not mean she has a burning desire to see you again.

On confidence. Yes, confidence is super sexy. No, you don't have to be a Brad Pitt or Tom Cruise, but if you own up to what you have, if you appear confident with who you are, it's a big turn on. R. Don Steele, the author of "Body Language Secrets: A Guide during Courtship and Dating" wrote (2), "This desire is evolutionary. Females want someone who's not going to run from a fight, a man who is confident in his ability to provide and protect." Very true indeed. If you do not feel it, it's time to do something about it. For starters, hit the gym more often; exercise has long been known to release endorphins, and get you back in physical and mental shape.

Ideally, on the first date you should be both interested in each other, asking questions reciprocally and getting to know the other side. This isn't a one-man podcast, so don't steal the show for the most part of the date. It is good to ask open-ended questions. Inquire about your date's job, books she's read, movies she's watched, travel plans. People love talking about travel, their past journeys, things gone wrong on holidays, the destinations they are planning to visit. Recently, in the times of the COVID-19 pandemic traveling has been limited, and people have compiled bucket lists and travel plans they want to talk about.

First date scene. You two are having brunch on Saturday morning, laughing and having a good time. And then, for some inexplicable reason, you decide to tell her how, during the strict lockdown in the infamous Covid-19 pandemic, you managed to smuggle yourself across the border to another country, just to see your ex-girlfriend and spend time with her. You might as well ask for the bill right there and then and call it the end. Yes, your first date girl is still sitting at brunch with you physically, smiling, laughing and making fun of your adventures, but inside she is disappointed that you are telling her about your ex-girlfriend, that you are showing her your keen interest in seeing your ex, even if it was "back then". Frankly, it makes one lose interest just like that. If you still miss your ex-girlfriend, then this is not the time to meet new women with the intention of dating and pouring your romantic memories onto them. Talk to your best friends, your mama or your therapist instead. Clear your head, and once you know you are more interested to get to know the woman sitting in front of you, rather than bathe in your goodtime recollections, then you have all the chances to make the date fun for both of you.

Case scenario for expats. You both are expats living and working in a country, both young and at the beginning of your career, trying to make it in the new place and make it your home. Your date tells you she is sharing a flat with a girl, who is a local in this country. You ask her jokingly "can you introduce me to your flatmate, ha, ha, ha". Watch her mentally delete your phone number and erase you from her present, and do not be surprised when you ask her out again on the second date, she says she's busy.

<u>The takeaway</u>: Let's settle this once and for all. If you are (somewhat) interested in a woman and fancy seeing her again, if you want to make a good impression, at no point in the conversation on the first date you mention your exes, her female flatmates or other women whatsoever. Period.

The bill. The controversial topic. Yes, we in the Western world want equal rights among men and women. But guess what, being a gentleman and settling the bill yourself on the first couple of dates will get you a lot further than in the otherwise case. Yes, we are strong and independent women, who enjoy our freedom and supporting ourselves, but every time you let us split the bill on the first dates, a tiny hope that you are a Prince Charming dies inside us. We won't show it of course, keeping on smiling and talking to you, but the level of interest towards you was just reduced significantly. Here is a top tip on how to attract your date in a coffee shop: let her ahead and get her to order the coffees for both of you at the counter. She is now wondering how you two are going to pay. Once the barista mentions the price, move her aside, step forward and pay for both coffees. Bingo, you are now the hero.

In fact, I believe the man settling the bill on the first dates actually supports the equal rights. We women spend a lot of money and effort on getting ready, on the nice clothes and designer bags, on the make-up and beauty treatments. The least you can do is buy a cup of coffee.

There are two cases when you are allowed to split the bill: 1) you are absolutely 100% sure you never want to meet this woman again or 2) she is a hardcore feminist, who looks like she is about to physically fight you.

Chapter 5:
Good manners and pickup

The key message: "*Good manners will open doors that the best education cannot.*" — *Clarence Thomas*

A fundamental rule of good manners is to give. Whether it is attention, support, interest, a compliment, or a gift. Please do show us that chivalry isn't dead. Having good manners is more than just holding the door open for a person next to you. It is about being a gentleman, respecting others and yourself, about doing acts of kindness and projecting good energy into the world. And it surely will not go unnoticed by a woman. Some men out there appear withdrawn, barely interested, yet still asking us out on dates. Had you been disappointed or hurt in the previous relationship, it is better to sort it out and let it go. No one appreciates a drag.

Smile. Smiling is the universal language, connecting people from across the globe. On the first dates and generally always, try to be in the good mood when meeting people. There is a saying "smile and the world does too". Smiling has actually been shown to be good for your health. It releases endorphins, it may lower blood sugar and blood pressure, boost your immune system, reduce stress and anxiety, as well as act on serotonin release and create your happy mood. So why not smile more often? Why do men occasionally appear tense and withdrawn on the first date? Do you expect us to entertain you? We aren't circus clowns. And entertaining should be reciprocal.

Be on time. You should always be on time on the first date. Being on time goes beyond simply having good manners. It is another act of establishing trust and showing whether others can rely on you. Being late on the first date shows how much you value and respect your first date (not too much clearly), and how well organized with your time you are (not so well apparently). It is a turn off for a woman to have to stand there for 5–10 minutes in front of the coffee shop/bar/whatever the location and wait for you. And the other way round, if you appear 5 minutes before the set date time, it's only bonus points for you, for being punctual and appearing in good shape.

Look at your date when she is speaking to you. A smartphone should not be anywhere in sight. Put it away. Making eye contact during the conversation is a vital social skill. Research shows the power of making and maintaining eye contact with the person you are talking to, has many benefits, such as people will be more likely to remember your face and what you said, long after the conversation is over (and you do want to leave a lasting good impression, no?). People will also be more inclined to believe what you are saying. You will be perceived as more confident and intelligent. Your date will be better able to read and mirror other non-verbal cues, which helps in establishing a connection. In other words, so many points for you from one simple rule.

Listen before voicing your opinion. Having an open mind and interest in what your date has to say shows respect and attention. Maintain eye contact, do not interrupt and listen carefully. Do not criticize, whine, nag or complain. As mentioned before and mentioning again, negativity in all forms has to be avoided (generally) and on the first date specifically. The first date is not the place to tell her you cannot afford your own real estate and you're not sure whether you ever will in this expensive city. She is not your financial advisor or a business coach. Spare her your gloomy thoughts.

On giving attention. People do not wish to lose their "cool" side these days. To many people it seems think it's better to appear busy, distracted and not to show their feelings towards the woman they would like to get to know more about. If you are interested in your match, do not be afraid to show more of your energy and good manners. While walking a woman home after the first date may not be possible (getting to know someone's home address at the first encounter can appear too personal), order her a taxi or walk her to the bus stop and wait at the bus stop with her, until the public transport arrives. If the date finishes late, do let her know you wish to receive a message from her to know when she gets home. Text to say you had a good time a short while after the date, instead of waiting two-three days.

Do pick up the phone and call to ask how she is doing. In the age when our smartphones are predominantly being used for any other purpose rather than making a call, stand out and dial her number. In 50 years' time, our smartphones may require an app to download in order to make a phone call and classes on 'how to have a telephone conversation' will be taught in schools, as we are so used to tapping away text messages, tweets and posting pictures on Instagram. However, until then, stand out, stop hiding behind SMS and emojis, and master that form of audio communication. Research has shown that people sense emotions more easily in voice-only conversations, thus talking on the phone actually helps to connect with each other. Use it to your advantage.

On being honest. People can often sense when you aren't being genuine. It is very much attractive and well mannered, if you can own your words and mean what you say, as well as say what you mean (well, exclude our sometimes-questionable fashion choices from here, I am aware that purple blouse is too tight, but it was on sale, okay?). When we have to read between the lines through garbled stories, we often start questioning how true you actually are and if we can believe what you say.

On generosity. Here is a second date story. Once a man took his date on a day road-trip into the countryside. On the way back after a whole day of driving, she asked him if he was still feeling okay to drive a couple more hours. He confirmed, and said she could take over, if she wants to.

"You would trust me with your Porsche?" she asked.
"Why not, it's just a car?" he replied.

One sentence was pretty much all it took, to completely sweep the girl off her feet.

Here is another dating story. Once a girl was learning

how to drive, and asked the guy she was dating if she could practice driving with him. His reply was the insurance only covers him as a driver. That was also pretty much all it took to completely lose interest.

Being generous does not equate to being rich and owning a luxury car that you aren't afraid to let others drive. It is about being a giving person, and being happy to share. A scientific paper published in Nature (3) found a neural link between generosity and happiness. The researchers used functional magnetic resonance imaging to show that generous behaviour increases happiness and motivates generosity. Thus, happy people are generous people and vice versa.

When defining generous behaviour, one could probably think of donating money to charity, or volunteering one's time to help the poor. And not everyone is inclined to invest themselves for the sole benefit of others. However, that is not all there is to generosity. It is not the same as pure altruism, and it is possible to be genuinely generous, serving one's own interests. When a man is being generous with things, whether it be possessions, money, time, attention, support, encouragement, emotional availability, his actions show his intentions towards the woman. Being generous goes hand in hand with being kind and friendly. And those are the qualities that attract women.

House visits and dinner parties
When you are just starting to date someone and she invites you over to her house, as a general rule, *do not* show up empty-handed. It's simply called having good

manners. Bring her a bottle of wine, a box of chocolates, a tea basket (on the first invitation), a takeaway dinner, a fridge magnet, a pretty cookie (later on). She will likely serve you drinks/food and yes, she is extremely happy to see you, but your mere presence is not a good enough contribution to the table. In the case you worked late and only remembered about her invitation at the last moment, and you are too lazy to stop at the nearest supermarket (read: it's a turn off), please consider not telling her "I wanted to bring you something, but then I forgot". You didn't forget to come over to dinner, darling, did you?

Good table manners showcase you in good light no matter whether you are dining out or staying in, whether in the company of you date or in the group of friends. Learn the basics of table manners and apply at all times.
- Wash your hands before meals (or even better, as soon as you enter the house). It is good etiquette and a good hygiene rule (especially in the times of a flu season or a pandemic).
- Put your phone away, and do not look at it at the table; you are here focusing on the person(s) in front of you.
- Do not speak with food in your mouth — a piece of tomato on a white shirt anyone?
- Use your utensils for the purpose they were implemented for — eating. Do not gesture with them.
- Avoid burping or making other rude sounds at the table.

For more thorough dining etiquette rules, such as the use of silverware, please consult extensive various sources out there.

If the food is being prepared during the dinner party, for example it is a BBQ, a pizza night, bonus points for you if you make sure the hostess also has food on her plate. If she is offering you a pizza slice, having a clean plate herself, while you already have food on yours, please do consider giving it to her instead. She is being a good host, making sure everyone is happy. An act of care from your side will go a long way. It would be nice if you offer your help with cleaning up after the meal. The next day following the dinner party, please do text to thank the hostess and let her know you enjoyed your time. Somehow, not so many people are aware of this small act of kindness and the good light it puts you in.

Chapter 6:
The dos and don'ts

Key message: "Shall we make a new rule of life from tonight: always to try to be a little kinder than is necessary?" — Sir James Matthew Barrie

This chapter is a summary outline of what has been discussed before and can be used as a general guide on how to approach women.

Online profile

The dos

Keep it simple and honest	The first step towards greatness is to be honest — Proverb.
Keep it real	No matter what you do, stand up for who you are as a person. Your name, age, photographs should be real and up-to-date.
Be friendly	A hello message in the profile description, a couple of smiley emojis
Do upload good content images	You are clearly visible, preferably showing off the winning smile in well-lit, sharp images.

The don'ts

Do not lie	About your age, your name, your job, your marital status, etc.
Do not whine	Stating how little you can offer to the future potential matches is a big turn off.
Do not appear depressed	Dating is supposed to be fun and easy-going. Do not expect your future date to be your therapist. If you are not feeling it, get off online dating and do something good for yourself instead.
Do not upload grey, blurry images	A picture is worth a thousand words.

Communication

The dos

Do call her by her name	As Dale Carnegie stated, "A person's name is to that person, the sweetest, most important sound in any language."
Be spontaneous	Aim to build a connection first without making sure she is looking for a relationship.
Do respect	Respect her, her time and her values.
Do inquire	Asking questions will show your interest. Ask how is she doing, how is her day, what is she up to on the weekend. Where was she on that cool photo wearing a beautiful black dress?

Think before complimenting	Do you really want to tell a young and beautiful girl in her late 20s that she is aging well like a good wine? Tell her she is gorgeous instead.
Do smile	Win her over with your charming, happy smile.
Do call	In the age when everyone is sending out text messages online, stand out, pick up the phone and call her.

The don'ts

Do not assume things based on short profile description	Do not assume who your match is, what she makes of her time, what she does or how she feels. Always ask a question instead.
Do not drag it out	If you like your match, *act* on it, arrange a date, make a phone call, let her know.
Do not tell us what to do	Whether it be the time we can come for a date, how we should behave, how we should feel, what should we eat and wear.

Dress-code

The dos

Do take care of yourself	Personal hygiene is of vital importance. The use of toothbrush and tooth paste, mouthwash, laundry detergent and perfume help greatly.
Dress your age	No ripped jeans with glittery T-shirts in the +30 category.
Invest in a watch	A watch will add visual points to any outfit. It can polish the look.
Do invest in high quality items	A couple smart casual outfits of high-quality fabrics will project a well-dressed image, and last a long time, unlike the low-quality mass-market clothing.
Do get clothes that fit well	Well-tailored suit specifically according to your shape.

The don'ts

Do not wear worn-out, baggy, stretchy clothes to the first date	Instead organize a few smart casual outfits that suit your age and style.
No flashy fabrics	Get rid of flashy suits, they look cheap.
No outdated trends	No speed dealer sunnies, no cargo pants, red/white ties with black shirts.

First date

The dos

Do be on time	Being on time helps to establish trust and shows respect for your date. It gives you time to take a breath and appear cool, calm and collected, and organized.
Do appear open and confident	Confidence is the one single biggest aphrodisiac. Own up to what you are and go out there.
Do appear happy	Project positive vibes, and the people around you will be happier too.
Be a gentleman	Open doors, help with a coat (ask beforehand, if you may help), ask her what she wants to do, settle the bill.
Be generous	With your attention and interest, with giving genuine compliments.

The don'ts

Do not be late	Please don't be late. It is a turn off as a woman to stand there in front of a bar and wait for the first date to arrive. It is implying either how little you care or how bad your time management skills are. Not good in either case. If you know you are going to be late, do message in due course, so your date is aware and can use the time to her needs.

Do not talk about your ex-girlfriend or your female friends.	Simply turn off. You are here to get to know more about the woman in front of you. If you talk about your ex-girlfriend on the first date, you are risking never seeing your match again. We are not your therapists. Get your ex back or get her out of your head before arranging dates.
Do not just talk about yourself for the duration of the date	A date is not a one-man podcast show. Do show interest in the other side.
Don't check your phone	Unless your job involves emergency services, there is no other reason why you cannot switch your phone off for a couple of hours.

Finale

*"Then came a moment of renaissance, I looked up —
you again are there, a fleeing vision, the quintessence of
all that's beautiful and rare."* — *Alexander Pushkin*

In the end, it all comes down to chemistry. As research shows, between 70 and 93% of all communication is non-verbal. We look at the way the person talks, rather than what he or she is saying. We are attracted to their voice, the way they smile and laugh, and hold themselves. The way they make us feel. We choose our partners based on their character and the mutual connection. However, to get to that stage, it is important to spark interest on the other side, show a good first impression, and establish trust. When you are feeling your best self, good things start happening.

In the event of the date not working out the way you'd hoped, and your match still not being interested in you, despite your best efforts, treat it as a business affair — it's not personal, accept the rejection, don't waste time and move on.

The takeaway. The key to getting the attention of a woman is simple. Be a gentleman, open that damn door. Kindness, good manners and a happy mood, that's all there is to it. Make her laugh and show your interest. The rest of the story is up to you, so make it a good one!

Bibliography

1. Morewedge CK, Giblin CE, Norton MI. The (Perceived) Meaning of Spontaneous Thoughts. J Exp Psychol Gen. 2014;143(4):1742—54.
2. Steele, R D. Body Language Secrets: A Guide During Courtship And Dating. 2003.
3. Park SQ, Kahnt T, Dogan A, Strang S, Fehr E, Tobler PN. A neural link between generosity and happiness. Nat Commun [Internet]. 2017;8(May):1–10. Available from: http://dx.doi.org/10.1038/ncomms15964

www.ingramcontent.com/pod-product-compliance
Lightning Source LLC
LaVergne TN
LVHW041549060526
838200LV00037B/1213